The Cameraman

Nalya Thomas

Published by Nalya Thomas, 2024.

THE CAMERAMAN

First edition. June 28, 2024.

Copyright © 2024 Nalya Thomas.

ISBN: 979-8227091635

Written by Nalya Thomas.

The Cameraman

By: Nalya Thomas

New Opportunity

The silence in the old house was short lived. Rain danced against the windowpane, a relentless drumming that did nothing to soothe the chills that ran up and down Clyde's spine. The grandfather clock audibly ticked and Clyde shot up when he heard a shrill cry. He looked around for the site of the news and his gaze locked onto his cellphone. When he glanced at the small screen he saw that it was three o' clock in the morning. "Hello?" he asked groggily, putting the phone to his ear.

"Clyde!" the woman on the other line cried. "What's wrong, mom?" the young adult asked tiredly. "The rug! Come check the rug!" she screamed in terror. Clyde threw his phone down, not bothering to hang up, before crawling out of bed and heading down the old wooden stairs that creaked with every step. He checked the living room rug and he was perplexed. A crease formed in his brow as he looked up at his mother and said "there's nothing here". "I know" the older woman smiled from the couch, "it's pretty". The woman looked at him innocently, her wrinkled face crinkling even more as she grinned.

They inherited the house from his grandfather when the man passed away from old age. The best way that he could describe the entire house was cozy. Almost everything in the house was brown and the firehouse and the exterior were decorated with brick. Every now and then Clyde would sneeze. The house was so old that there was dust and mold in places that they couldn't reach. His room especially gave him the creeps when they first moved in. There was a large grandfather clock that ticked audibly and he couldn't sleep for the first few nights that they moved in. Now, he wasn't phased by the noise.

Clyde laughed and shook his head in disbelief. He ran a hand through his messy brown hair as he sat beside his mother. He'd have to get ready for work soon anyways so there was no point in going back to sleep. The woman was currently looking through a family photo album. "Look at your cute little baby butt" she smiled. Clyde laughed at the woman's odd comment and flipped the page. "I didn't wake you, did I?" she asked worriedly. "No, I was already awake," he lied. Her worried face turned into a smile.

"I'm making pot roast for dinner today" she grinned.

"What's the occasion?" Clyde asked.

"Your uncle is coming over today," Sharon smiled.

"Ah, he's a handful," Clyde said, causing his mom to laugh.

"He always brings you gifts though," Sharon said, ruffling her son's hair. Sharon's hair was brown as well but it was a lighter shade and graying at the roots. Her green eyes fixed on her son and she smiled. His brown eyes met his mother's and he shared her grin.

"What do you want for breakfast?" Sharon asked.

"Aww, you don't have to cook for me, mom," Clyde laughed, "I'll just have cereal".

"Nonsense" Sharon argued before insisting, "I want to cook for you". Clyde laughed and said, "pancakes, eggs, sausage, bacon and your famous cinnamon rolls". Sharon nodded and said, "I'll get started on that". She gave her son a wet kiss on the cheek before getting up and fleeing to the kitchen.

When his mother wasn't looking, Clyde wiped his cheek and cringed. He'd have to focus on his cheek when he washed his face. He got up and headed to the bathroom. He ran through the shower, brushed his teeth and washed his face. After getting dressed, he headed into the dining room. His father was sitting at the dining room table reading a newspaper. "Hey kiddo" Paul grinned, looking up from the paper.

"Who's that?" Clyde asked, pointing at a woman that was on the back of the newspaper. Paul turned the paper around and laughed before asking, "do you like her?". Clyde nodded. "She's a reporter in Florida," Paul explained. "I wanna go to Florida," Clyde gushed. Paul laughed while Sharon turned her attention from the eggs that were scrambling and she said, "be careful with those journalists, son".

"That's where your uncle works," Paul said.

"Has he ever mentioned her?" Clyde asked hopefully.

"Well, he's an executive so he doesn't visit the station often but the few times he has met her, he's had nothing but negative things to say about her" Paul admitted.

"What does he complain about?" Clyde asked as a plate of food was set in front of him.

"She's just rude. A primadonna bitch" Paul said before covering his mouth and snapping. "That's a dollar in the swear jar" Sharon told her husband as she served him her breakfast. "I thought it was a quarter" the man grumbled, reaching into his pants and pulling out his wallet.

After Clyde finished eating, he bid his mother and father goodbye before hopping into his car and driving to his job. He headed into the private photography studio. He said good morning to everyone before heading into his room. He checked his appointment book before setting up his equipment.

After a few minutes, an attractive blonde came into the room.

"Hi, you must be Elanore," he smiled.

The woman nodded.

"So what kind of photos are you taking today?" the man asked. "Boudoir," she answered sweetly. Clyde smiled and ran a hand to his brown hair. He silently praised God before asking the woman if she had any reference pictures.

On his last client of the day, he saw that face again.

"Who's that?" he asked.

"Cora S. Pondent" the redhead grinned, "she's my idol".

"Is she?" Clyde asked.

"She's a boss bitch" the woman said, causing Clyde to burst out laughing. "That's a dollar in the swear jar" he teased as he analyzed the reference image.

Cora had big brown eyes that looked innocent. Her hair was dark brown and her skin was pale. Her plump lips were bubblegum pink and she had long, black eyelashes that almost touched her cheekbones when she blinked. Clyde ran his finger across the woman's lips in the photo. "Ahem" the redhead coughed, bringing him back to the real world. "Sorry" he blushed before asking, "can I pay you for this picture?".

When Clyde left work, he hurried back home. He didn't want to risk not seeing his uncle when so much was at stake.

"You're home early" Sharon mused before saying, "your dad is still at work".

"What's that amazing smell?" he asked.

"Fresh brownies," Sharon smiled, "they're cooling on the counter". Clyde nodded. He waited on the couch and twiddled his thumbs until there was a knock on the door.

He excitedly ran to open the door. Damien, Paul's older brother, stood at the door wearing a big grin on his face. The gray haired man ruffled Clyde's hair before giving his nephew a hug. "Come in, come in," Clyde urged. Damien made himself comfortable and kicked his shoes off. He let out a groan in frustration. "What's wrong?" Clyde asked. "I have a dilemma," the old man said dramatically. "What is it?" the younger of the two asked.

"I urgently need a cameraman," Damien sighed.

"Where?" Clyde asked.

"Down at the station," the man sighed.

Clyde bit back a smile. He couldn't seem too eager or the man would be skeptical and question his intentions.

"Oh, that sucks," Clyde said, not really meaning it.

"I know, we need to find someone last minute," Damien hissed, lighting a cigarette.

The smoke caused the fire detector to go off and Sharon scolded them before telling them to go outside.

"What happened to the last cameraman?" Clyde asked.

"He died" Damien said, to see his nephew's reaction, before laughing and saying, "he quit. They all quit".

"Why are they quitting?" Clyde asked.

"Because they can't put up with Cora. She's so fucking awful, I wish they would fire her already" Damien complained.

"I can take the position" Clyde volunteered.

"I don't want to put that burden on you," Damien said.

"I insist. I've always wanted to live in Florida. That gives me a good excuse" Clyde said.

Damien thought about it before patting his nephew on the shoulder and saying, "if you promise you won't quit, the job is yours".

"I promise," Clyde grinned. Damien looked conflicted. "I'll see what I can do" he told Clyde before saying, "if I can get a yes. You need to move fast. Pack your stuff today". Clyde grinned before running inside and upstairs to his room

(Not-So) Humble Beginnings

Clyde wiped the fog from his mirror as he danced. It was bright and early Monday morning. His uncle had gotten him the photographer position and they'd driven together to Florida. Clyde danced as he brushed his teeth and hummed. He rinsed his mouth and spit. There was a knock on the door so Clyde went to answer it. Damien stood outside smoking a cigarette. "Wanted to say goodbye before I flew home," the man smiled. Clyde nodded. When Damien went for a hug, Clyde pulled back. "I'm naked," he argued, gesturing to the towel. Damien scowled and said, "I changed your diapers when you were a baby". Clyde laughed before hugging the man. "Good luck on your first day. Knock them dead, tiger" Damien said before getting into his taxi and leaving.

Clyde headed to his closet to get dressed. He parted his clothes like Moses did the Red Sea, revealing the picture of Cora that he'd bought from his client. He sighed and caressed the picture, giving it a kiss. "We'll meet today, my love" he whispered before he finished getting dressed. Once he was dressed, he put his equipment in his car before driving down to the station. When he got to the building he took a deep breath before spraying himself with cologne and popping mint gum into his mouth. He grabbed his backpack of equipment and headed inside. He headed through security and took a deep breath before knocking on the door to the recording room.

A tall man with blonde hair opened the door. "You must be the new kid" he smiled before extending a hand and introducing himself, "I'm Preston Katz". "Donovan. Clyde Donovan," Clyde smiled, shaking his hand. He was invited in. "This is the new guy," Preston announced. The recording and audio crew all choroused hellos while the meteorologist came over. "I'm Seth Storm" the meteorologist greeted. "Pleased to meet you," Clyde said politely.

Seth retreated after saying hello while Preston sat and chatted with him. The best way that Clyde would describe Preston was charismatic.

Everyone chatted and laughed, the room was loud until the door swung open. The entire mood changed and everyone fell silent. Clyde heard the clicking of heels approaching the door.

Cora S Pondent walked past the door in all her glory. Her brown hair was bouncy and she had a confident aura. Today she was wearing a blue blazer and skirt outfit. Her voluminous hair was wavy and her makeup was beautifully done. Clyde whistled as she entered the room. He b-lined to her and before he could introduce himself she said, "I don't give autographs at work".

"He's the new cameraman," Preston said, rolling his eyes. "Oh" Cora said, eyeing Clyde up and down. "Obviously" Cora scoffed before asking, "why else would he have a backpack?". Cora looked Clyde up and down and a small smirk tugged at her lips. "How tall are you?" She asked with a hand on her hip. "Six foot two" Clyde answered before asking, "how tall are you?". "Guess" she said with her arms crossed over her chest. "Five foot two?" He asked.

She rolled her eyes and said, "I'm five foot four". "Big difference," Clyde teased. She flipped him off before taking his glasses and trying them on. "You can't see at all," she laughed. He smiled at her antics. "Cora, stop being a whore" Preston scolded. "How am I being a whore?" she asked, taking the glasses off and pushing them into Clyde's chest. "You flirt with every new hire that comes in here," Preston said. "No, I don't," Cora said firmly. "I don't appreciate you calling me a whore" she said, her small body shaking with anger.

"Then stop acting like one," Preston shrugged. "Dude, don't call her that" Clyde said, standing up for her. "You don't know her like I do" Preston said, "if you did, you'd stay far away from her". Cora got pissed and stormed outside. "She probably went to cry," Seth teased, causing everyone except for Clyde to laugh. Preston handed him a stack of papers and gave him a key to the company truck. "Cora can't drive for shit-don't let her drive" Preston advised.

When Clyde got outside, Cora was standing outside of the van. "He unlocked the vehicle and opened the door for him. She avoided eye contact with him. She was staring down at her lap. "Hey, I don't care what Preston says" he told her, trying to comfort her. "For your information, I don't give a damn about what you or Preston think about me" she hissed, her tone full of venom. "Where do I drive?" Clyde asked. "To the park" Cora said, dabbing a tissue under the corner of her left eye. "Uh" Clyde said sheepishly, "I'm new here". Cora sighed in annoyance and gave him the verbal directions.

When they arrived at the park, she touched up her makeup before getting out of the van. "Focus on my left side, it's my good side," she told him. "Every side is your good side" Cldyde smiled. She didn't even crack a smile, her little smirk that she had in the studio was long gone. She had a poker face on and said, "tell me when you're ready to roll". "I'm ready," Clyde told her, aiming his camera.

"My name is Cora S. Pondent and I'm signing off with Channel Five News". Clyde stopped rolling and she sighed. Her professional smile that she had on quickly fell. "What are you getting for lunch?" Clyde asked. "I don't eat lunch," she said curtly. "Why?" Clyde asked innocently. "I don't have any money," she sighed. Her arms were crossed over her chest and she was avoiding eye contact with him. "I have money" he offered before asking, "what are you craving?". "I don't need your fucking money" Cora spat, walking away. He followed behind her and said, "I insist". "I want fork food," she sighed.

Clyde surveyed the area and landed on an asian restaurant. He got teriyaki chicken with fried rice while Cora got orange chicken with white rice. He had a sweet tea while she ordered a lemonade. "Thank you" Cora said softly before saying, "I'm sorry I was rude earlier". "It's okay," Clyde smiled. "How does the orange chicken taste?" she asked. He pushed his plate towards her. She smiled and stabbed a piece with her fork. "It's good but a bit spicy," she laughed.

"So where are you from?" she asked. "Alabama," he answered. "Do you have any siblings?" she asked. "No, I'm an only child," he answered nonchalantly. "So no sisters I should be jealous of" she teased with a laugh. He was confused until he understood what she was saying and laughed. "That's tough talk coming from a gator wrangler" he said, causing her to giggle. "I've actually never seen a gator before," she whispered. "Same with incest in Alabama" he smiled. She giggled and he was about to reach out and touch her hand until she checked her watch and said we have to go.

After she finished her second broadcast for the day, she smiled. "It's such a nice day today" she cooed. "It really is" he agreed before asking, "would you like to take a walk with me?". "Are you asking me on a date?" she teased. Clyde blushed and was flustered. "W-w-well I mean.." he stammered but he was cut off when she said, "if you are, I'm not that easy". She punctuated the sentence with flipping her long hair in his face . He gulped and nodded before he asked, "can I walk you to your car?". "It would be your honor," she smiled. He walked her to her car and watched her drive away before he headed over to his own car.

"Hey, new kid!" Seth called out to him. Clyde halted and turned around. "What's up?" he asked. "Wanna go for drinks?" Seth asked. "I don't swing that way," Clyde said, causing his co-worker to burst out laughing. "Good one" Seth smiled before saying, "seriously though, I wanna get to know you. Dissect your brain a little bit". Clyde wanted to say no but he did have questions about Cora that he wanted answered. "Sure," Clyde agreed. The duo decided to meet at a nearby bar.

Loose Lips Sink Ships

"On me" Seth smiled, offering his bank card and paying for the first round of shots.

"So where ya from?" Seth asked.

"Bama," Clyde answered simply.

"Roll Tide" Seth said, pumping his arms.

"Thank you," Clyde laughed.

"So what'd you graduate with?" Seth asked, throwing back a shot of whiskey.

"Bachelors of arts" Clyde answered, taking a long swig before saying, "I also have a business degree".

"Nice" Seth nodded before saying, "Bachelors of science. I majored in atmospheric science".

"Sounds hard," Clyde cringed.

"Eh, it's not too bad," Seth shrugged.

"So, are your parents together?" the older of the two asked.

Clyde laughed, "polite way of asking if I'm a bastard. But yes, they've been happily married for twenty-eight years".

"And you're twenty eight I'm assuming?" Seth asked.

Clyde nodded before asking, "how old are you?".

"Guess" Seth teased.

"Forty?" Clyde asked mischievously.

"Fuck you" Seth said, flipping him off before throwing back another shot.

"Well?" Clyde asked.

"I'm thirty-two" Seth hissed.

"And how old is Cora?" Clyde couldn't help but ask.

"Twenty-five and Preston is thirty".

"So what's the story between those two?" Clyde asked.

"Wouldn't you like to know?" Seth teased. Seth sighed and paying for another round of shots he said, "they used to date".

Clyde stared at him, hoping that he'd say more.

"Cora was, like, sixteen. He was twenty-one. She's always been smart, she was a prodigy taking college classes..." Seth trailed off and threw back another shot.

"Why'd they break up?" Clyde asked.

"He dumped her because she wouldn't put out , so she begged him to get back together and she slept with him. She asked if they could date again, he said no and she attacked him. It's how she got her domestic violence charge..it only recently got expunged off of her record".

Clyde's blood boiled.

"So he took her virginity and dumped her? Then he called the police on her?" he asked.

Seth nodded and said, "it was a cunt move. But he apologized. Cora is vengeful though, she always holds grudges".

Clyde frowned and asked, "is she single?".

"Yeah, far as I know, she hasn't dated since having her heart broken," Seth shrugged. He pulled out his phone and showed Cora's mugshot. She had mascara running down her face, her lipstick was smudged and her hair was a mess. *Coraline Smith booked for domestic violence and battery.* She looked so broken in the picture. She was also sporting a busted lip and a shiner where he assumed Preston hit her.

"Her name is Coraline?" Clyde asked.

"Yep, don't refer to her as that though" Seth told him, "she hates it. It reminds her of her past...". "She's never had anyone love her," Seth said suddenly.

"What do you mean?" Clyde asked.

Seth was so tipsy at this point that he was slurring his words. "Her whore of a mother cheated on her dad, after suspicions and a DNA test he packed up shop and left them. Her mother and brother were pissed and she claims that they're abusive" Seth shrugged before saying, "my brief interactions with them they seem like good people. I think Cora's just jealous".

"Why would she be jealous?" Clyde asked.

"Because Connor is a doctor while she's a failed reporter" Seth laughed.

Clyde nodded before asking, "Connor's her brother?".

"Yep. He's always donating to local charities. When she had to interview him one time the tension was so thick that you could cut it with a knife". Seth tried to order more drinks but he was cut off. He got belligerent with the bartender before Clyde calmed him down.

"Do you think Cora likes me?" Clyde asked.

"Yeah, she's not as cordial with everyone else. I can tell she thinks you're cute" Seth answered before saying, "she loves tall guys with brown hair. The icing on the cake is someone that can make her laugh".

"Have you ever tried to get with Cora?" Clyde asked.

"No," Seth said, shaking his head, "she's too immature for me. She's so fucking childish. And she's the textbook definition of a narcissist, she always wants her ego stroked. She's also just delusional. She thinks she has so many fans when most people around here don't even know who the hell she is".

"So if I made a move it wouldn't cause any problems?" Clyde asked. "Not with me" Seth answered before saying, "Preston doesn't want Cora but he doesn't want anyone else to have Cora either".

"Fucking toxic" Clyde complained.

"I'm just telling it like it is," Seth shrugged before yawning and saying, "I think I'm gonna call it a night. I'll see you tomorrow".

Mommy Dearest

"And this is Cora S. Pondent signing off with Channel Five News" Cora sung. "So what are you doing after work today?" Clyde asked. Cora sighed and said, "I have to run some errands". "Can I come with you?" Clyde asked. "If you're paying," Cora teased. Clyde grinned. He got into his car and followed behind hers. The duo drove to a nearby grocery store. After Clyde opened the door for her, Cora said, "last one there's a rotten egg". Before he could react, he saw her running into the store.

He laughed as he chased behind her. "Not fair," Clyde argued, "I had to close the door first". "So?" Cora asked, giggling like a schoolgirl. Clyde smiled down at her. Today the duo had subs for lunch. "So what's the plan?" Clyde asked, pushing the shopping cart. "Just getting some groceries," she smiled. Clyde nodded. "Do you think it would be a fair race now?" she asked. "I think so," Clyde laughed. "Race you to the milk" she said, pushing the cart back before she ran. Clyde ran to the dairy section and he almost beat her until he bumped into someone.

"Shit, I'm so sorry" Clyde apologized, helping the guy that he knocked down. "What the fuck" the man in green scrubs cursed. Cora came over and explained, "it was an accident". Clyde looked between the two and connected the dots. This must be Connor. Connor stared at Cora while her gaze fell to the ground. "How do you know her?" Connor asked. "I'm her co-worker," Clyde answered. Connor stared at him before shaking his hand and introducing himself, "I'm Connor. I'm a doctor and her big brother". "Nice to meet you," Clyde smiled.

"You can't speak?" Connor asked her.

"I said I'm sorry" Cora said softly.

"You haven't visited mom lately" Connor said, staring at her.

"I just haven't had time," Cora said.

"But you can play in the store?" he asked.

"I'm grocery shopping," she argued.

Connor was quiet before asking, "why are you dressed like a whore?". Cora felt subconscious and put her hands over her low cut top.

"She's not dressed like a whore" Clyde argued, "she's dressed how she wants to dress".

"Which is like a whore" Connor laughed.

"You must be her boyfriend," Connor said, looking Clyde up and down. "What if I am?" Clyde asked. Connor laughed and said, "you're not but if you were, I'd say you're a downgrade from the last one". "Leave him alone!" Cora yelled. "What was that, pipsqueak?" Connor asked, advancing towards her. Cora screamed and put her hands up in defense but Clyde got in between them and pushed Connor back. Connor's head knocked back against the glass door to the freezer. "Go visit mom" he spat to Cora before he pushed his full cart to checkout.

Cora looked at Clyde and asked, "will you go with me to visit my mother?". "Of course" he reassured her. After they finished grocery shopping, he followed her to her mother's house. Cora grabbed the yellow magnolias that she got for her mother and took a deep breath as she walked up to the door before she knocked. An old blonde opened the door with a cigarette in her hand. "I got these for you, mom," Cora said, offering the flowers.

"Where are my cigarettes?" the blonde asked, not accepting the flowers. "I didn't get you any" Cora said as she was let inside. "Who the hell is this?" the woman asked, looking Clyde up and down. "He's a friend from work, mom," Cora said softly. "It's a pleasure to meet you, Ms Smith," Clyde smiled. "I wish I could say the same," the blonde sneered. "You don't ever send me money like Connor does," the woman complained. "I don't make as much as Connor either" Cora argued.

The house was in a general state of disarray and roaches crawled on the walls and floor. "Fuck, that was my last cigarette" the blonde complained, putting it out underneath her heel. Clyde cringed and he shuddered from the filth. "You got that news gig and now you think you're too good to be associated with your mom" the woman accused.

"It's not that, I don't have the time" Cora sighed, "my job comes with a lot of research and fact checking". The blonde laughed before saying, "you don't do anything but stand there and look pretty on camera". Cora hugged herself as she quietly looked at her mom.

"Go get me some cigarettes" the blonde commanded. "No," Cora said softly. "Excuse me?" the woman asked. "I said no," Cora said defiantly. "No? You don't tell me no" the blonde hissed, standing up from her chair. "Sit the fuck down" Clyde told the woman as she began to approach Cora. "I'll call my son to kick your ass," the woman threatened. Her teeth were oddly shaven as if she wore veneers in her youth and her fake breasts almost touched her navel. "You're gonna let him talk to your mom like that?" the woman asked in a raspy voice.

"No, mom," Cora sighed. "Get up and talk to me face to face" the woman said, picking up an empty shot glass and throwing it at her daughter. "You're done," Clyde said, standing up and pushing the woman down into her chair. She screamed at the top of her lungs as if he was attacking her. "Get the fuck off of me!" the elderly woman yelled. "Cora, go get in the car" Clyde commanded. Cora stood up, unsure who to help. "Cora, go get in the damn car" Clyde yelled. "You're gonna let him hurt your poor mother?" the blonde asked raspily.

Cora stood up and gently pried Clyde's hands off of her mom. "You go wait in the car" she said softly. "Are you sure?" he asked. She nodded. He didn't go to the car. He waited outside the door. "What the fuck was that, Cora?" the woman asked. "He was just trying to protect me," Cora sighed. "From what?" the blonde spat. "From you" Cora answered. That enraged the woman and she stood up. She punched her daughter in her left eye before she grabbed the brunette from the hair.

"You think you're too good, bitch" the woman hissed, slapping her daughter a few times in the face. "Stop it," Cora cried. "Shut up" the blonde screamed, striking her again. Everytime the blonde hit her daughter, her rings cut the young woman's face. Cora slapped her mom and the two started to scuffle. "You're gonna hit your mom, bitch?" the woman asked. Cora let out a scream and Clyde burst through the door. He pulled the women apart and scolded the blonde, "you failed as a mother and a wife".

Comfort and Cuddles

He grabbed Cora and helped her out to the car. He pulled her into his car and drove away. "We'll come back for your car" he promised. He didn't think that she was in any state to be driving. They drove to his place and he carried her inside. When he set her on his couch, she burst into a fresh set of tears. Salty water and blood poured down her face. "I don't know why she hit me" Cora sobbed as Clyde gently wiped her face with a paper towel. She had a few small cuts from when she was hit with the big rock on her mother's ring.

"I don't know why she hurt me," Cora cried. Clyde hugged her as he applied small bandaids on the cuts on her face. "Is it bad?" she asked. "No, it should be healed by Monday" he promised her. He wrapped her in his arms as she sobbed into his shoulder. "I'm not a bad girl," she cried. Clyde gently pushed her back and wiped her face. "You're a good girl," he told her. She nodded as she wiped her own face. "Can I kiss it better?" he asked. She cracked a small smile for the first time in the hour and nodded.

Clyde gently pressed kisses all over her face. She winced in pain but after a while she relaxed. She wrapped her arms around his neck and hummed in content. "What would make you happy?" he asked. "Some food" she answered after thinking for a moment. "What are you craving?" he asked. "Pizza, tacos, burgers and sushi" she decided. Clyde nodded and rubbed her back comfortingly as he ordered delivery. "Should be here in about an hour" he said before asking, "do you wanna take a shower before it gets here?". She looked down at her blue blazer that had snot, blood and tears on it and nodded.

He followed her into the bathroom as he started the water for her. Then she followed him to his closet. He tried to block her view but he pushed past her and she saw that he had a picture of her taped to the wall. "What is that?" she asked with her arms crossed over her chest. She didn't look bad though, the same smirk that she had the first day she met him was playing on her face. "It's nothing," he said, covering the picture and handing her a shirt. It was a basic, white t-shirt that his mother had bought him for Christmas and it was a size too big on him so he knew that it should fit her like a gown.

She looked up at him and smiled. Even after she grabbed the shirt, she prolonged the eye contact. He looked down at her and cautiously smiled. "Do you like me?" she suddenly asked. He felt like his heart was going to explode. "It's a simple question," she shrugged. He just stared at her, unsure what to say. When he didn't answer she giggled and shook her head. She disappeared down the hall and into the bathroom. Clyde cursed, hoping that he didn't just mess things up.

When he went down the hallway, he saw that she left her discarded clothing outside of the bathroom door. He picked up the clothes and headed into his laundry room. He threw her blazer and skirt into the washing machine before he looked down at the garments in his hands. The brunette had been wearing black, lacey bra set. He put an ear to the wall and listened to the shower water running. He decided that she should be there for a while. He clutched her panties in his right hand and brought the garments to his nose.

When he left the laundry room, his heart was pounding and his fair skin was flushed. "Sounds like you were having a good time with the washing machine" she teased. Cora's hair was damp and she must've put the shirt on while her skin was still damp because the white shirt had the t-shirt look and it left nothing to the imagination. "Oh, you heard that?" he asked sheepishly. "Yeah, I think I even heard you say my name," she said with her arms behind her back.

Before he could confirm or deny, there was a knock on the door. He opened the door and it was their delivery. He brought the food inside and she led him to the bedroom. She crawled into his bed. He got into the bed and opened the food. Cora grabbed the remote and flipped through the channels while Clyde unboxed the food. He got one drink while Cora got two. He got soda while she had a milkshake and a lemonade. They had pizza, burgers, sushi and tacos.

"Thank you" Cora smiled adorably as she munched on a taco. "No problem" Clyde smiled before pretending to yawn and wrapping his arm around her. Cora snuggled into his shoulder as she ate. "Yes," Clyde said suddenly. "Huh?" Cora asked, looking up at him. "The question you asked me earlier" Clyde elaborated, "the answer is yes". Cora smiled and she leaned up and gave him a kiss on the cheek. "Do you like me?" he asked. "I don't know yet" she smiled sadly. He nodded, considering everything she'd dealt with in her past he didn't mind her being cautious.

"What's your dream day?" he asked. She closed her eyes as she sipped her shake and said, "going to the aquarium and having orange chicken" she smiled, "going shopping afterwards and coming home to cuddles and a nice massage". Clyde nodded. When Cora's gaze was focussed on the romcom playing on the television, Clyde grabbed his phone and purchased two tickets for the aquatic theme park the next day. He also booked their reservation at the asian restaurant at the park.

"Pay attention to the movie," Cora hissed, playfully slapping his arm. Clyde kissed her forehead and nodded. "That's gonna be us one day" he commented, pointing at the couple kissing on screen. Cora stared up at him and burst out laughing. "Is that a no?" he asked sheepishly. "It's a we'll see," she smiled. Clyde moved his arm from her shoulder to her waist. He hugged her tightly and the duo cuddled until she fell asleep. Clyde stayed awake for a few hours to watch the brunette peacefully sleep before he set an alarm and fell asleep.

Saturday Day Fun Day

Cora woke up in the morning to the sweet-hickory smell of pancakes and bacon. The brunette stirred awake and was surprised to see Clyde standing in front of her with a plate of pancakes, eggs and bacon. "Breakfast in bed?" she asked. "I wanted to surprise you," he shrugged. "Well I'm definitely surprised" she smirked as the glass plate was placed in her lap. "I have a lot of fun stuff planned today" Clyde said as he sat on the edge of the bed.

"My feet are killing me from wearing heels yesterday," she said suddenly. Clyde was confused as to what that had to do with the conversation topic. It took him a minute before he asked, "do you want me to rub them?". "Is that even a question?" she asked, reaching over to the nightstand and grabbing her glass of orange juice. Clyde chuckled and shook his head before he removed the blanket from her feet and began to massage her left foot.

"So what are we doing today?" she asked. "Theme park" he smiled. There was a knock on the door and he excused himself. He returned to the bed with a few packages and tore them open. "I wasn't sure what you'd like so I got you a few outfits" he smiled. Cora grinned up at him. After eating, she decided on a cobalt blue skin tight t-shirt with denim daisy dukes. She also wore a pair of white sneakers that he bought her. They were a size too big but, with her feet already working and all of the walking they'd be doing around the theme park, that was preferable.

After Clyde got dressed he put the plates in the dishwasher before they headed to the theme park.

Clyde loved the way Cora's eyes lit up once they got to the entrance of the park. He giggled and massaged her hand that he was holding. He paid for her parking and then they headed to the parking lot. They got onto a tram and were driven to the entrance. Thankfully, it wasn't too packed as far as theme parks go. Clyde grabbed Cora's hand and headed to guest services. After activating their tickets, they headed to the ticket line. "Long line" Cora complained. "You're not used to waiting?" Clyde asked. "I don't wait," Cora snapped. Clyde laughed.

Unlike how she usually wore her hair down on the news, today she had her hair in a bun with a butterfly clip. "I guess I should buy the pass to skip the lines, huh?". She nodded her head. He laughed and they headed back to guest services before he they finally went through the ticket line. "So what first?" Clyde asked as she grabbed a map. "I want to see all the shows," she told him. "Okay" Clyde agreed. He checked the app on his phone and saw what times the shows were happening. He set alarms so that they could see the shows on time and get good seats.

"Let's do the penguin ride," Cora suggested. Clyde nodded and they headed to the ride queue. "It's cold," she whispered. Clyde rubbed her arms comfortingly. "Better than the heat outside though" he replied. "I guess so," Cora agreed. "How many?" the employee asked. "Two," Clyde answered. Him and Cora were led into another room. "I can see the ride from here" Cora said excitedly. "Me too," Clye smiled. It was adorable to see her jump and down like a bunny.

After a few more minutes, they were led into the ride vehicle. "Does this spin?" Clyde asked. "Uhuh" Cora nodded as they were locked in, "it's not scary though". The cold was long forgotten when the ride began to spin wildly. "Not scary," Clyde laughed. "I mean," Cora shrugged with a smile. The ride juxtaposed learning material with a fun ride. There were no dips or drops. They just spun around a flat floor. "That was fun" Cora smiled when they got off.

"What now?" Clyde asked. "Can we get a snack?" she asked. Clyde nodded. He scanned the park and asked, "do you like hot dogs?". She nodded. The duo headed over to the snack cart and got hot dogs and drinks. "Do you order lemonade everywhere you go?" he asked. "Is that a problem?" she teased. "No, I was just asking" Clyde laughed before teasing, "it makes ordering for you easy". Cora blushed and hid her face in his side. He wrapped his arm around her and after they discarded their trash it was time for the first show.

They entered the large stadium and Cora frowned. "Where are the orcas?" she asked. "They haven't been let in yet" Clyde told her. They sat near the bottom of the bleachers as she said that those were the best seats in the house. Clyde had to admit, they did have a pretty good view but he was worried about being in the splash zone. Cora comforted him saying that they could dry off by going on a coaster afterwards. After a few minutes, the orcas were let into the other side of the water. Cora let out a scream in delight.

Clyde had an arm wrapped around her as they hugged. "This is the best day ever" Cora whispered before giving Clyde a peck on the kiss. "Thank you," she grinned. Clyde touched the side of his face as he blushed. They watched the orca jump, twirl and dance. The crowd all screamed in delight. "We need a volunteer for this next part," the blonde female employee announced. Cora immediately shot up like a rocket. "Me! Me!" Cora screamed jumping up and down. Clyde stood up and yelled at the top of his lungs. The worker looked over and said, "the woman in the blue". Cora screamed and headed up to the water.

Clyde pulled out his phone and started recording. "What's your name?" the worker asked. "Cora. Cora S Pondent" Cora said proudly. "Oh, you're the reporter," the blonde said as she recognized her. The worker turned to the crowd and laughed, "we're gonna be on the news". Cora did a spin and the orca spun as well. She did a few more movements and the orca mimicked her after the trainer gave the command. The final move that the worker had Cora do was wave. The brunette screamed when the orca waved and splashed her with water. Everyone laughed and the trainer gave Cora a high five.

"Did you get that?" Cora asked with a smile when she returned to her seat. "Yep," Clyde smiled, showing her the footage. Cora squealed and wrapped her arms around him. Clyde blushed as he brought his arms to her lower back. "You heard she recognized me?" Cora gushed. "Of course, you're a local celebrity" Clyde told her, pressing kisses to her uninjured cheek. Cora batted her eyelashes and flipped her hair. "I'm a celebrity?" she asked, grinning. "Yup, and I'm your biggest fan" he told her, grabbing her hand and kissing it. The show ended shortly after and everyone in their section was soaked.

"Doesn't that one go upside down?" Clyde asked as they headed to a roller coaster queue. "Yeah but you're lying on your stomach. It's not bad" Cora smiled, "it's my favorite ride". Clyde secretly prayed as they put their stuff in the free locker. "Are you scared?" she teased, a smirk tugging at her lips. "Maybe" he said before asking, "are you gonna let me hold your hand?". "I guess I'll let you hold my hand" she said dramatically as if it was inconveniencing her. She held out her hand and he intertwined their fingers as they entered the line.

"Ready?" she asked him as they were locked in. Clyde was used to harnesses but he never had to have his legs locked in. "Why are our legs restrained?" he asked. "So we don't fall out," Cora smiled. Clyde let out a yell in surprise when the employee hit a button and they were now lying on their stomachs. Clyde took a deep breath and squeezed Cora's hand as they slowly went up the lift hill. He glanced at Cora and saw that she had a grin on her face. He couldn't help but smile at how happy she looked.

His smile quickly dropped with the ride. "Fuck" he cursed. Next thing he knew they were flipping, twirling and dropping. The ride was over in less than two minutes but it felt like forever. Clyde squeezed his eyes shut as they hit an inversion. Next thing he knew, the ride abruptly stopped. "Are we done?" he asked. "Yeah" Cora smiled. Her hair was wild and she was giggling. "That was exhilarating," she smiled. Clyde let his breathing calm as they were put back into a seated position before the restraints were released.

"No more coasters for the day" he told Cora as they retrieved their stuff from the lockers. Cora giggled and wrapped her arms around Clyde's left arm. "Let's go through the shark tunnel" she squealed. Clyde sighed, knowing that they were in for a long day. He stared lovingly at the brunette as she pulled him hard by his arm. After traversing the shark tunnel, they made their reservations and rode a few more motion simulators before going home.

Cora sat in Clyde's bed and sighed. He was currently in the bathroom getting the shower water started for her. When he returned to the bedroom, she looked up at him lovingly. "What's up?" Clyde asked. She picked up her orca plushie and pressed it to his lips. "He wanted a kiss," she smiled. Clyde giggled and ran a hand through her hair. "The water's ready," he told her. She held eye contact with him before getting up and heading into the shower.

Clyde looked through his closet and picked out a sports jersey that he used to wear back in high school for her to wear. After a few minutes, a gust of heat hit the hallway and Cora emerged from the bathroom. Her hair was damp and she had a towel wrapped around her. "Hey" Clyde smiled, offering the jersey. Cora accepted the jersey and dropped the towel. Blood went to Clyde's face and groin at the display. She put the jersey over her head before crawling into his bed.

Clyde crawled into bed beside her, wearing nothing but his pajama pants. Cora was rubbing the side of her face. "What's wrong?" Clyde asked. "It itches," she giggled. "Want me to kiss it better?" Clyde asked hopefully. Cora rolled her eyes before smiling and agreeing, "sure". Clyde opened his arms as an invitation and she straddled his lap. He pressed kisses all over her cheeks and forehead. Cora giggled and wrapped her arms around his neck. "Does that feel better?" he asked. "Yeah" Cora smiled before bashfully saying, "you missed a spot".

Clyde was confused until Cora crawled off of him and dramatically yawned. "I'm calling it a night" she loudly announced as she turned on her side. Clyde watched her for a few moments before he gently turned her over. He leaned over her and captured her lips with his own. When he pulled away to see her reaction, Cora pulled him down and kissed him again. The duo made out until they were both breathless. Clyde rested his forehead against hers and a string of saliva connected them.

"So does that mean you like me?" Clyde asked. "Maybe" Cora shrugged before she threw a pillow at him, promising that they'd talk in the morning. She used the excuse that she was too tired to have the conversation at the moment. Clyde frowned and he heard her sigh. "I don't do relationships" Cora said, her voice suddenly full of venom. "Why?" Clyde asked as he massaged her arm comfortingly. "Everyone I've ever been in a relationship with has hurt me," Cora said sadly.

"Will you let me be the exception?" he asked. Cora was quiet before she sat up and said, "get on your knees and beg me. Maybe I'll consider it". Clyde dropped onto the floor, pulling the blanket off of the bed in the process and got onto all fours like a dog. "Not like that" Cora laughed, "do it like your praying, like your begging. Clyde pushed up so that all of his wait was on his knees. He clasped his hands together and pleaded, "Cora, please, will you date me?". "Why should I?" she asked, a hint of amusement in her tone. "Because I want to treat you good. I want to cherish you, baby. I want to spoil you. I want to wake up to you every morning and sleep beside you every night...I want to passionately make love to you and kiss you. I want to start a family with you". He stood up and grabbed both of her hands, looking into her eyes seriously as he asked, "so what do you say?". "Yes," Cora agreed, standing up and kissing him.

Eviction Day

When Cora woke up, she was greeted with French toast. The bread was sprinkled with powdered sugar and the plate was garnished with strawberries and blueberries. "Oh lala" Cora grinned. She sat up and clapped her hands happily. "What's the plan for today?" she asked, grabbing her fork and digging in. "We need to get your car and then grab your stuff so that you can move in with me" Clyde told her, kissing her left hand. "Moving in already?" Cora asked with a smile. "Yep" Clyde grinned.

After she finished eating, she dressed in a graphic t-shirt and baggy pants. She put on a baseball cap and sunglasses and then she was ready to go. The duo went to Cora's mother's house to retrieve her car. All four tires were slashed, the windows were broken and profanity was graffitied all over the car. Cora stared at her car in disbelief. "Call the fucking police" she said angrily. Clyde called and within minutes, officers were on the scene. They didn't even need to take statements. The car and the cuts on Cora's face were evidence enough.

The officers took the pictures and told the young couple that they would stay with them while they waited for a tow truck to come. After about half an hour, Cora returned home. "What the fuck" she screamed, getting out of her car and going to attack her daughter. When the cops tried to arrest her, she spit on and attacked them. The older woman was promptly tased and apprehended on charges of: domestic violence, battery, assault, drunk driving and vandalism. The woman screamed and kicked as she was put into the back of the police vehicle.

Once the car was towed to the dealership, the couple headed to Cora's house to retrieve her stuff. Cora gasped when she saw a paper taped to her door. She snatched the paper off and sighed when she read it. "What's it say?" Clyde asked. "I need to be out by the end of the week" she sheepishly admitted. Clyde nodded and said, "well at least you were going to live with me anyways". She smiled at that and pressed a kiss to his cheek.

The duo headed inside and Clyde felt like calling it a studio apartment was a stretch. The whole thing felt like it was the size of a walk in closet. They packed the entirety of her bedroom into the car before driving back to Clyde's place. Cora sighed as she unpacked. "Are you okay?" Clyde asked. She nodded and said, "that place just brings back bad memories, can you just bring everything over for me?". He nodded and kissed her forehead.

Sibling Rivalry

"My name is Cora S. Pondent and I'm signing off with Channel Five News" Preston mimicked before asking, "what happened to your face?". Cora looked crestfallen. "We have wild sex" Clyde said, standing up for her. Preston's face fell and he sneered at Clyde. "Really?" Preston asked, silently seething and balling his fists in anger. Preston looked like he wanted to say something to Clyde but he simply stomped out of the studio.

"You fucked up, dude" Seth said, shaking his head. Seth left but they never heard the door close. Instead they heard footsteps approaching. Cora's heart nearly stopped when she saw Connor. Today he was wearing blue scrubs and a scrub hat. "What the fuck, Cora?" Connor cursed before angrily ranting, "first you attacked mom, then you put her in jail and now Preston just told me that you fucked this chump?" "I didn't" Cora told her older brother.

"You liar" Connor hissed, throwing a camera at her. "Stop it" Clyde said warningly. "Or what?" Connor asked. "You assaulted my mother and then you defiled my sister" Connor yelled at Clyde. "Shut the hell up" Clyde said rolling his eyes, "I never touched your bitch of a mom. And as far as Cora is concerned, she can do whatever the hell she wants. She's an adult". Connor was seething. Cora screamed and curled into a ball as Connor advanced towards Clyde.

"You son of a bitch" Connor hissed, throwing the younger male against the wall. Clyde punched the older male and kicked him. The two began to throw down, knocking over recording and sound equipment. "Stop it!" Cora screamed, covering her ears. "It's not my fault you want to fuck your sister" Clyde said, causing Connor to temporarily stop his assault. "What?" the doctor asked. "I see how you look at her," Clyde said, wiping blood from his mouth before spitting on Connor's scrubs. When Connor advanced again, Clyde grabbed a tripod and knocked the surgeon out.

"C'mon" Clyde told Cora, helping her up. Tears rolled down her cheeks and she was shaking with fear. "I thought he was going to hurt me" she sobbed into Clyde's chest. Clyde went to call the police but she stopped him, her reasoning was that he wouldn't be able to work with a criminal record. Clyde reluctantly agreed and drove her home. Clyde sat on the closed toilet seat while Cora treated his cuts and bruises. Her phone kept vibrating. "Who is it?" Clyde asked. "It's Preston" Cora said, looking down, "he said he's going to ruin my life".

"Were you two dating?" Clyde asked. "We did," she admitted, "but not since I was a teen. I don't know why he's acting so jealous". Clyde shook his head and promised her, "no matter what curve ball gets thrown your way, I'm going to help you and be there for you". "Thank you" she smiled, pressing a washcloth covered ice pack to his swelling cheek. She caressed his hair and sighed before she hugged him. "We're in this together" she smiled sadly. Clyde nodded. No matter what obstacle came their way, he'd help her through it.

Deadline

The next day after work, Cora entered the station bubbly with a bounce in her walk until she saw Bobby. Bobby was one of the CEO's and he didn't look happy to see her. "Hi Bobby," Cora greeted. "We need to talk," the older man told her simply. Clyde tried to follow behind her but Bobby stopped her and said, "I only want to talk to Cora". Throughout the duration of the meeting, the young woman was chewed out and scolded for Connor tearing up the studio and told that she'd be cited for the damages.

"I didn't tell him to come," Cora argued.

"But you also didn't call the police on him," Bobby, one of the CEO's, argued.

"Because I don't want him to lose his license" Cora sighed.

"Even if that is true, your ratings are low" Bobby sighed, "we might have to let you go".

Tears rolled down Cora's cheeks as she asked, "is there anything I can do?".

"You have two options" Bobby told her, "you can either have a story for me by Friday or if you meet me for dinner tonight, we can ensure you a spot at the station". The older man's hand traveled to her knee and he squeezed her thigh. Cora screamed and stood up. The older man looked at her and laughed. "Don't be stupid" he told her, "I can make or break your career. So what will it be?". "I'll have a story by Friday" she told him, tears and mascara running down her face. "If you change your mind, you know my number".

"What did he say?" Clyde asked when Cora got into the passenger seat of his car. "I need to go to dinner with Bobby," Cora said, wiping her face. "For what?" Clyde asked. "So I can keep my job" she said, bursting into tears. Clyde's blood boiled. "You're not going to dinner with that old fuck" he told her. "I don't want to lose my job," she sobbed. "He didn't give any other options?" Clyde asked.

"I need to have a story by Friday" Cora said, "which is impossible. Stories don't just fall out of thin air. It takes time". She sniffled and tried to stop crying but more tears rolled down her face as she explained her predicament. "I'll find you a story" Clyde promised, wiping her wet face. "How?" she asked him. "I'll find a way," he told her, "you won't lose your job. I'll make sure that won't happen". When they got home, Cora went to sleep. She denied dinner and watching television as she just wanted to lie there.

When Cora was sleeping, Clyde decided to go for a walk to clear his mind. He dressed himself in all black; sweatpants, sneakers, gloves and a hoodie. He rummaged through his bedside table and pulled out his hunter knife that his uncle had got him when he was a teenager. He put it in his hoodie pocket and kissed his sleeping girlfriend on the cheek before he left.

When he arrived at the park, he began to walk around the lake. He took a deep breath and sighed. His brain racked as he thought about different stories that he could pitch, the problem was they all required a lot of research. He put his hoodie on when he was hit with a cold breeze. He let his eyes close for a moment and his mind began to wander until he heard screaming. He got up and went to the site of the noise.

He saw a man assaulting a woman. Her clothes were strewn about and the man was on top of her. The man was dressed in all black and his teeth were clamped down on the woman's neck. He also held a knife to the other side of her throat, pressing it warningly against her carotid artery. Clyde was pissed. "Get off of her!" he yelled. The man temporarily turned around and when he did, the woman kicked him. She grabbed her clothes and attempted to run away. Unfortunately the man caught up to her and dragged her back by her leg.

The woman screamed in terror. Clyde walked up to the man and pulled out his hunting knife. He quickly jumped the man and slit his throat. His body fell limp and the blonde was able to run away. "Thank you" she told him, tears rolling down her cheeks, before she retreated.

Clyde stared down at the man. He couldn't help but smile at the rush he got. He was a hero. He'd just saved a woman's life. He was a fucking martyr. He put a bloody hand to his chin and thought about it. This would make a good story idea. He analyzed the scratches on the man's arms and the woman's discarded panties.

He could see the headline now: good samaritan killed a rapist in self-defense to protect a woman. That was fun but no one would have reason to continue watching if the threat was eliminated. He thought of a more fun twist. What if there was a serial killer? Everyone would be glued to the news because they'd want to know where the killer would strike next and who the targeted demographic was.

Clyde nodded and stabbed the man a few more times. He stabbed the man until his head was almost decapitated and his internal organs were exposed. Clyde grabbed the man's intestines and wrapped them around his neck. Clyde grabbed the girl's panties and stuffed them into his pocket before he hid the man's body in a nearby bush. Clyde hurried home and discarded the panties into the outside trash can. He then threw his clothes in the washing machine before starting the shower water.

"Babe!" Cora whined. Clyde entered the bedroom wearing nothing but his underwear. "How long have you been calling for me?" Clyde asked. "I just woke up," the brunette whined before asking, "why are you taking another shower?". "Cold sweats," Clyde answered. Cora scrunched her nose up in disgust. "You do stink," she agreed. Clyde laughed and said, "yeah, I'm about to shower". "Hurry up. I want cuddles" she demanded. Clyde laughed and kissed her forehead.

Red Herring

When Cora and Clyde entered the studio in the morning, Seth and Preston wouldn't speak to them. Clyde wordlessly got the keys and they got into the van. "I wanna go downtown," Cora suggested. "I think the sunlight will be better in the park," Clyde told her. Cora nodded as she adjusted her lip gloss. When they got out of the van, Clyde started rolling and led her to the bush. "What's that?" he asked when she didn't notice it. Cora's mouth hung open in shock and she covered her mouth. "Are you getting this?" she asked. Clyde nodded.

"Oh my god" Cora said, looking at the macabre scene. She took out her phone and called the police. She sat down on a wooden bench nearby and Clyde recorded her reaction. He recorded her interaction with the cops and the crowd that surrounded the body. Clyde concealed a smile, he knew that this would bring in ratings. Everyone looked terrified. Some people were crying, others were screaming but everyone looked distressed. Nearby, a little girl started crying. Clyde continued rolling as Cora bought the little girl a double scoop vanilla ice cream cone with sprinkles. "You're such a sweetheart," Clyde smiled. Cora simply smiled.

After work, the couple met at a restaurant. "That was crazy in the park today," Cora said, stirring the straw to her margarita. "Yeah, definitely have to drink after seeing that," Clyde said, massaging his temples. He had three shots and a margarita. "I haven't thrown up since I was a kid" Cora said, "and seeing that shit made me throw up". "It's okay" Clyde comforted her. "Whoever did that is still out there" Cora told him. "I'll keep you safe," Clyde promised, kissing the back of her hand. Cora cracked a smile at that.

"I guess so" she said before telling him, "we'll have to check out the park tomorrow to see if the Organ Strangler is out tomorrow". "Organ Strangler?" Clyde asked. "Yeah" Cora smiled. "Maybe the next killing will be more tame" Clyde mused, "we don't know his MO yet". "His?" Cora asked, raising an eyebrow. "Their" Clyde corrected, "I just can't see a woman being so vicious". "You've met my mother" Cora said, causing Clyde to giggle. "Touche" Clyde smiled, throwing back his last shot before starting to drink his margarita.

Clyde's heart ran cold when he saw the woman from last night staring at him. She had a thousand yard stare and she looked at him as if she remembered him. "Do you know her?" Clyde asked Cora. Cora glanced at the woman before smiling and saying, "she's probably one of my adoring fans". Cora wrote her autograph on a napkin and handed it to the frail woman. The woman looked at Cora in confusion before she fixed her gaze on Clyde and muttered "thank you". With that, she left. The words sent chills down Clyde's spine, it was the same words uttered to him that fateful night.

Cora sighed before saying, "it's sad that someone died but this will bring in ratings, for sure". She looked around before quietly whispering, "is it bad that I hope they strike again?". "Not bad" Clyde told her, "you're being more logical than emotional". She giggled and smiled at him before saying, "I hope Preston is one of their victims". "What about Connor?" Clyde mused. "Him too. And my mother" she said, wiping her mouth with a napkin. After she wiped her mouth, she threw the napkin at Clyde and he caught it.

The giggling duo left the restaurant after he paid and went home. "Want some tea?" he asked her, "It'll help calm your nerves". She nodded as she got ready for bed. When she was comfortable underneath the thick comforter, Clyde came into the room with a mug of green tea. "My favorite" she smiled up at him. "I know," he grinned. She drank the tea while they talked. Everytime she sat it down, he coaxed her to drink more. This happened until she finished the mug and after about half an hour she was knocked out cold.

Hero

Clyde returned to the park with his usual getup, this time wearing two pairs of gloves and a mask to conceal his identity. He went to the park and hid in the bushes as he waited for a deserving victim. It took hours until a family came to the park. A nuclear family in every sense of the word; a mother, a son and a father. Clyde watched the woman take a nap on the bench while the dad and son played. Clyde turned his attention elsewhere but the family grabbed his attention again until he heard screaming.

He turned back around when he heard the child screaming. He peeked through the bushes and saw the father beating the son with a leather belt. The redhead got up from the bench and began to try to stop, who Clyde assumed was, her husband. Her attempts were fruitless and it only made the man attack her too. "Get off of my mommy!" the little boy screamed, attacking his father's legs. When Clyde crawled towards them, he saw the boy's pale skin not only had red welts from the belt but both of his eyes also had shiners.

Clyde tackled the man and began to stab him. "You abusive son of a bitch" Clyde hissed. He stabbed the man so hard that the knife bent. The young boy hugged his mother's leg and looked down at Clyde. "It's okay" the red haired woman comforted her son, "it's all over". The woman approached Clyde and reached into her pocket. She pulled out a twenty dollar bill and told him, "you're our hero". Clyde didn't accept the money. He didn't want to speak as it would give off who he was so he simply waved the mother-son duo away. The woman didn't linger a second longer, she simply smiled at Clyde before running away.

Clyde hit the man in the lake before heading home. He was giddy. He was a hero. That made him happy. He flew down the road but when he headed home, he saw the lights were on. His heart stopped. He took off his bloody sweater and gloves before he headed inside. "Where were you?" Cora asked with her arms crossed over her chest. Her eyebrows were furrowed and her lips were in a thin line.

"Hey, babe, I just went to get gas," Clyde shrugged. "It couldn't wait till morning?" Cora asked, getting up and approaching him. "Let me check your phone," she demanded. "Of course," Clyde said, handing it to her. She looked through the phone and after she was done, she threw the phone aside and smiled up at him. "Come here" she told him with open arms. Clyde hugged her and pressed a soft kiss to her lips. Cora smiled at him and rested her head on his chest. "Why is your heart racing?" she asked. "Just excited to be around you," Clyde smiled.

"Yeah? I excite you?" Cora asked huskily. "Always," Clyde said, kissing her again. The couple made out and Clyde let his hands wander to his girlfriend's backside. Cora giggled against his lips. "You make me so excited, babe," Clyde told her when they pulled apart. "Let's take this to the bedroom" she whispered in his ear. Clyde picked up her, relishing how she squealed in delight at how strong he was. "You don't seem like the gym type" Cora giggled when she was gently tossed onto the mattress. "I'm athletic in other ways" he winked as he began to disrobe.

"So I guess this is the part where you leave me" Cora sighed, looking over at him. "No, this is the part where I ask you to cuddle," Clyde told her. Cora giggled and turned on her side so that they could spoon. "I love you" Clyde told her, kissing her neck. "I love you too," Cora smiled. "What kind of wedding do you want?" Clyde asked her, taking her aback. "What?" Cora asked. "What kind of wedding do you want us to have?" Clyde asked. Cora turned onto her back and sighed. "Part of me wants a big wedding and make it a huge media affair but another part of me just wants a quiet courthouse wedding with a glamorous honeymoon". "Well, think about it," Clyde told her. "Why?" Cora asked, "do you plan on marrying me?". "Maybe" Clyde said, giving her a soft kiss.

Big News

"Good morning from Channel Five News with Cora S. Pondent" Cora sang. "Today, a reporter gets engaged on air?" she said in confusion, reading the teleprompter. She watched Clyde set the camera down onto a tripod before he came into the camera's view. He got onto one knee and pulled out a black, ring box. "Will you marry me?" he asked. "Oh my god" Cora said, covering her mouth. She dropped her microphone in shock. "Well?" Clyde asked. "Yes, yes, a million times yes" she grinned, jumping up and down.

Clyde slid the big rock onto her finger before he picked her up and kissed her. "Back to our regularly scheduled programming" she laughed as he set her down, handing her back the microphone. "Let's see if the killer struck again" Cora said, heading over to the bush from yesterday. She didn't see anything. Her disappointment was visible on her face. "Check the lake," Clyde suggested. She didn't want to get her heels wet so she took the camera from him while he went into the murky water. He pulled the limp body out of the lake. Cora gasped in horror and disgust. She quickly made a call to the authorities and warned everyone to avoid the park.

"Fuck all that bullshit" Preston said angrily, "I'm gonna go to that park tonight and really see what's going on". "That's not smart" Cora told him, "a serial killer is running around". Preston laughed and asked, "do you hear yourself? Do you think we're supposed to cower in fear and avoid the park because of a supposed killer?". When Cora didn't answer, Preston laughed. He shook his head in disbelief and left. "What a dumbass," Clyde hissed. "If he dies, I'd get to be an anchor" Cora swooned. Clyde thought about it and realized that she was right. If he got rid of Preston, him and Cora would work inside the station.

After work, the couple went dress shopping. "So did you decide?" Clyde asked. "I want to get married at the courthouse as soon as possible," Cora told him, squeezing his hand. Clyde nodded and kissed her. "What kind of dress do you want?" he asked her. "Something simple," she smiled, "thigh high". Clyde nodded and asked, "do you wanna get married this weekend?". "Takes weeks" she sighed. "Let's go to Vegas," Clyde shrugged. "Okay" Cora smiled, swinging their interlocked fingers as they skipped together.

They walked around the different stores until Cora stopped in front of a white mini dress. "This is the one," Cora said, grabbing the dress. They also got white heels and a veil. Clyde paid for their plane tickets online. "You're booking first class, right?" Cora asked. "Yes, of course," Clyde laughed, kissing her cheek reassuringly. "We'll leave for Vegas after work on Friday" Clyde told her, holding all of her items and heading to the car. The couple headed home and Cora began to pack her bags.

"It's a few days away," Clyde laughed. "Never too early" Cora told him, "I hate last minute packing". Clyde nodded and asked, "would you like some hot chocolate?". "Please" Cora said before adding, "with marshmallows". Clyde nodded and headed to the kitchen. He pulled out a small pot and boiled some milk. He reached into the cabinet and pulled out a packet of hot chocolate mix and a bar of milk chocolate. He cut up the candy and dropped it into the pot.

He cut up and added a few sleeping pills. He stirred everything together before pouring it into a mug. He dressed up the treat with whipped cream and marshmallows. Clyde took the hot chocolate to the brunette. He watched her take a sip, laughing at her whipped cream mustache. "How is it?" he asked. "So good," Cora smiled, "and not too hot. The whipped cream and marshmallows help cool it without watering it down".

Clyde nodded and ran his hands through her hair. He helped Cora pack before giving her a nightgown to change into. After changing into a nightgown, Cora crawled into bed and turned on a romantic comedy. Clyde cuddled her and waited for the medicine to kick in. After a few minutes, she was already yawning and slurring her speech. Clyde kissed her forehead and snuggled with her until she fell asleep.

Once she was fast asleep, Clyde got dressed and headed to the park. He hid in the bushes and waited for Preston to arrive. He clutched his knife in his hand and tried to calm his breathing. It was too exhilarating. He just needed to knock out Preston, then he could go after Connor. He laughed maniacally before clasping his hands over his mouth. He mentally scolded himself for laughing. After about an hour, Preston arrived at the park. "Come out!" Preston yelled, "I'm all by myself".

Clyde crept up behind the blonde and stabbed him in the back. The stab was shallow and barely pierced skin. Preston threw Clyde over his shoulder and when he went to remove the mask, Clyde stabbed him through his hand. "Fuck" Preston cried. Clyde pulled the knife out and stabbed his other hand. "Who are you?" Preston asked. "I'm your worst nightmare" Clyde said through his voice distorter. He watched Preston shake in terror. Clyde pounced on top of him and stabbed him in the stomach. He tried to stab Preston in his heart but Preston threw him off and ran away.

Clyde chased behind him, slicing him with the knife. "Help me!" Preston screamed. Clyde clasped a thick gloved hand over Preston's mouth and tried to slit his throat. Preston bit down on Clyde's arm and ran away. Clyde heard footsteps in the distance approaching. He ran away and ran a few blocks away to his car. He headed home and hurried inside. He was anxious. He didn't finish the job. He headed into the bedroom and saw Cora still sleeping soundly. He kissed her forehead before he threw his clothes in the wash and cleaned his knife. He needed an alibi. He headed out to a local gas station. He bought a pack of gum before he headed back home and went to sleep.

Survivor

When Cora and Clyde arrived at the station in the morning they saw Bobby. "Cora, we need you to take Preston's place today" Bobby said with a grim look on his face. "Why?" Cora asked, biting back a smile, before asking, "how are the ratings?". "The ratings are good" Bobby sighed before saying, "Preston got attacked last night...at the park". Cora frowned and said, "I told him not to go out there". "I know" Seth sighed, "he went out there anyways and got stabbed over a hundred times. Thankfully, most of the cuts were shallow". "Did he at least bring a camera?" Clyde asked.

"No, the dumbass went out there with no camera and no weapon" Seth sighed. "We need to check on him," Cora told Clyde. Clyde nodded and agreed, "yeah, we'll check on him after work". Seth and Bobby both looked distressed. Clyde tried his hardest to maintain a poker face. "My name is Cora S. Pondent and I'm signing off with Channel Five News" Cora smiled. After work, Clyde said goodbye to everyone in the station before he took her to the hospital to visit Preston. They stopped at a grocery store beforehand to bring him flowers.

Cora picked out a beautiful bouquet of daisies. She clutched it tightly as they headed through security. "We're here to visit Preston Katz," Cora informed the woman at the front desk. The woman phoned Preston and he gave the okay to let them in. They were both given guest passes and escorted to Preston's room. "Hey," Preston said. "Are you okay?" Cora asked before saying, "I got you flowers". "You're a doll," Preston smiled. Clyde felt jealous but didn't say anything, he felt the circumstances were excuse enough. "Smell them," Cora said sweetly, putting the flowers in Preston's face.

Preston immediately began to cough and sneeze. "Cora, I'm allergic to daisies," he argued. "Oh, are you?" Cora asked innocently before saying, "I forgot". "Take those out of here!" Preston yelled. Tears welled up in Cora's eyes. "I just wanted to be nice and surprise you" Cora said, laying the flowers on Preston's face as she cried. "It's okay," Preston told her before apologizing, "I didn't mean to yell at you". Cora burst into tears and said, "you don't like them". "I do," Preston told her. He grabbed the flowers and sniffed them. "I love them," he promised.

Cora looked down at him and caressed his face. She looked at Preston and asked, "will you take these and wait for me outside?" she asked. Clyde sneered but agreed. He figured that being bed bound Preston shouldn't be too much trouble. Clyde gave Cora a kiss while making eye contact with Preston before he left.

"I have something to tell you," Preston said, grasping Cora's hand. "What?" Cora asked. "I think your boyfriend is the one who attacked me" he told her seriously. Cora furrowed her eyebrows and asked, "what?". "I think it was Clyde" Preston repeated, "he had this sinister look when I first saw him". Cora sighed and let go of his hands. "Why do you say things like that?" Cora asked sadly. "Cora, I'm serious" Preston told her, "he tried to kill me".

"What proof do you have that it's him other than him giving you an odd look?" Cora asked, as tears welled in her eyes again. Preston reached up a bandaged hand and wiped her damp face. "Clyde's trying to kill me," Preston told her, tears rolling down her face. "I don't have proof," he admitted, "but I know it's him. And if he wasn't fucking you every night, you'd know it's him too". Cora looked down at Preston and sighed. She got up and advanced towards the door.

"Cora, I love you" he told her. She turned around and sucked in a breath. "I'm engaged," she told him, showing off her ring. "Cora, if that's what this is about, I'll marry you" Preston told her. "I don't want to be in a loveless marriage with someone who looks down on me" she snapped. "Cora, I've never looked down on you and I never stopped loving you" he said, extending a hand out to her. Cora just stared at him and remained stagnant. "We're getting married this weekend," Cora told him. "Cora, he's a sociopath," Preston told her.

When she started to walk away Preston called out, "Coraline!". "Don't call me that" she hissed, turning to face him. "Set up a hidden camera. You'll see him leave every night. Or track his location" Preston told her. Cora shook her head defiantly and went to leave. "Check his arm" Preston told her, and with that she left. When she made it out of the front door to the hospital, Clyde stood there waiting for her.

"Let me see your arm," she said suddenly. "For what?" Clyde asked. "Just let me see," Cora said, reaching for his arm but he shrugged out of her grasp and knocked her onto the pavement in the process. "Why are you acting fucking crazy?" He yelled, looking down at her. "Stay away from me," Cora said softly. "What?" Clyde asked. "Stay away from me!" She screamed.

Clyde rolled his eyes and said, "Cora, let's go home". "Stay away!" Cora screamed, kicking him. "I'll show you my arm" he told her, holding out his hand to help her up. Cora reluctantly took his hand and accepted help up. "I'm sorry for yelling" he apologized before explaining, "I was just jealous". "Jealous of what?" she asked. "You and Preston, I know you like him more than me" Clyde said, tears rolling down his cheeks.

"Your arm," Cora said. Clyde rolled up his sleeves. "What happened?" Cora asked, pointing at a bite mark he had. "Stressed so I bit myself," Clyde told her. "Don't do that" Cora sighed before saying, "him and Connor are friends. I have to go tell him".

Doctor Dead And Dearest

The duo went to Connor's doctor's office but the nurses told them that he'd gone home early. Cora gave Clyde the directions to Connor's house. "Wait out here" she told Clyde, getting out of the car, "I don't want you two fighting". Clyde nodded and watched as she walked up with the daisies that Clyde didn't want. After a few minutes, the white door opened.

"What do you want?" Connor asked. "I brought you these because I have bad news" Cora told him, grabbing one of his larger hands and leading him to the couch.

"What happened?" Connor asked her. Today he was wearing black scrubs. The half-eaten sub on the table was evident that he had just come home for lunch. "Preston was attacked last night at the park" Cora said sadly.

"Why would that dumbass go out there?" Connor asked. "Because he wanted to catch the killer" Cora sighed, "but he didn't bring a weapon or camera". "What a dumbass," Connor laughed. His smile faltered when he saw Cora's sad expression. "I'm sorry about the other day" Connor told her, extending his arms. "It's okay" Cora smiled, accepting the hug. "I like this little dress you have on" Connor told her, tugging at the hem of the dress.

Cora smacked his hand away but didn't break the hug. Preston shoved her down onto the couch and pulled the dress up. Before Cora could scream, he clasped a hand over her mouth. "Don't scream" he told her warningly as he attempted to pull down her panties. Cora watched with tear-filled eyes as he began to untie his scrub pants. "Fuck, I've waited for this day for a long time, Cora" the man murmered, littering her neck with sloppy kisses.

Cora tried to kick and swing at him but he was too strong. "It's really your own fault" Connor rambled once he got his pants and underwear down, "you come into my house with flowers wearing a short dress that barely covers your ass and giving me 'fuck me' eyes". Cora stared at her older brother with terror in her eyes. She bit his hand so hard that it drew blood and she was able to temporarily scream before his hand wrapped tightly around her throat.

"Stop fighting, you know you like it" Connor said, positioning himself in between her legs. Before he could insert himself, the door swung open and Clyde was attacking him. "You sick fuck" Clyde cursed, punching the man. Cora made herself decent before running outside.

"What the fuck" Clyde cursed, choking Connor the same way he was choking Cora. He didn't let go until the man lost consciousness.

When Clyde came outside, Cora was sobbing and a spot in the grass showed that she'd thrown up. She was shaking with fear. Clyde held her and said, "let's get out of here". Cora nodded as she wiped her face. Clyde grabbed her hand and kissed it as they drove home. When they arrived home, Clyde picked her up bridal style and carried her inside. He set Cora down on the couch before he ran her a warm bubble bath.

While the water filled up the tub, he went to the couch to comfort her. He pulled her into his arms and hugged her. He peppered kisses all over her damp face and said "I'm sorry I wasn't there to stop him". "It's okay" Cora told him, "you saved me". She was still softly crying and he rubbed her back. "I feel dirty," she complained. "You're not dirty" Clyde told her, "it's not your fault. He's a sick fuck and he'll get his karma".

"Do you really think so?" Cora asked, looking up at him. "I know so," Clyde told her, kissing her forehead. "Ready for your bath?" He asked her. She gave a small nod before saying, "I want you to stay with me". "I will" Clyde promised, kissing her hand before carrying her to the bathroom.

After her bath, Clyde made her his special hot chocolate. She sat, towel-clad, in his lap as she drank it.

Clyde ran his hands through her hair and peppered her soft, damp skin with kisses. Today they have cartoons from her childhood playing on the television. "I love you" Clyde told her, pressing kisses to her soft cheeks. Cora looked up at uim and sweetly said, "I love you too". They spent the rest of the evening cuddling until she fell into deep sleep.

Clyde shook her a few times to make sure the drugs had taken their effect before he got dressed and headed to Connor's house. He didn't bother being discreet. He saw Connor watching television on the couch and broke through the living room window. Connor let out a scream in terror. "Shut the fuck up!" Clyde said through his voice changer, pointing a gun at the older man. "What the fuck?" Connor asked in fear, holding his hands up. Clyde knocked him out with the gun.

When Connor came to, he was tied to a chair and his mouth was gagged. He struggled and tried to scream but it was muffled. Clyde laughed and caressed the man's face. "Don't scream" he warned him, removing the gag. "Who are you?" Connor asked. Clyde didn't answer. Hr simply said, "you're going to receive your comeuppance for what you did earlier". At that point Connor's look of terror turned into a smirk.

"Clyde, you don't have the balls to do anything. Stop this little charade and untie me" Connor laughed. Clyde decided that his cover was already blown so he took his mask off. He reached into his pocket and pulled out his knife. "Tell me" Clyde said, slowly approaching, "how did you feel trying to rape your sister?". Connor rolled his eyes and said, "she wanted it. She was wet". Clyde's blood began to boil but he took a deep breath to calm himself down. He wasn't going to let Connor get away with a fast death, he was going to drag this out as long as possible.

"Which do you want to go first?" Clyde asked, "your fingers or your dick?". When Connor's eyes widened with terror, Clyde asked, "maybe that lying tongue?". "Stay the fuck away from me!" Connor cried, thrashing about. Clyde decided that he'd cut off Connor's dick. He gagged the man before pulling his penis out of the hole in his pants. Connor struggled but he froze with fear when he felt the cold blade against his manhood.

"Ya know, Cora didn't deserve what you did to her" Clyde said before commenting, "maybe I would've let you off easy if you were sympathetic". Even with the gag, it was the loudest scream that Clyde had ever heard. "Shhh, it's okay," Clyde smiled. With every cut and tear, Connor struggled even more. Tears rolled down his face. Clyde looked up and made eye contact with him as he made the last cut.

"I wonder what your mom is gonna think when she finds this on her doorstep" Clyde commented. Connor was hysterical at this point, sobbing and screaming through his gag. He thrashed and withered but he was tightly restrained. Clyde removed the gag and asked, "do you want to apologize?" "Fuck you" Connor spat. Clyde shook his head slowly before smiling. He was going to prolong this as long as possible. He put the gag back on the doctor and discarded the dick on the floor before he headed into Connor's room.

He began to look around for medical equipment. He needed something that would keep the man alive. He needed to prolong the suffering. He found an IV bag, pole but he didn't know what to put in it. He wheeled the equipment out to the study. Connor looked at it and shook his head. Clyde removed the gag and asked, "what do I put in here?". "Fuck you" Connor cried, tears and snot rolling down his face.

Clyde grabbed his gun and pistol whipped the man in the same spot. He watched the blood run down his face. "I was trying to help you," Clyde shrugged, knocking the pole down. "Untie me" Connor demanded, "I won't tell anyone. Just untie me. Let me go". "No," Clyde said simply. His eyes were dark and his lips were pressed into a tight line. "You'll be dead by sunrise," he promised.

Connor burst into a fresh set of tears. "I gave you chance after chance to redeem yourself" Clyde said, tugging Connor's head back by his hair, "but you were too damn stubborn". He pulled the gag up and began to decide what to remove next. "I don't think it was very nice how you choked my fiance" Clyde frowned, taking the knife and focusing his gaze on Connor's left hand.

"You know they say left-handed people are bad luck" Clyde mused as he began to saw the middle finger. "Shut the fuck up!" Clyde snapped, removing the finger entirely, "I'm sick of your crying". He removed each finger one by one until he had collected ten. A pile of blood was all over the chair and floor. "I'm sick of looking at your sad mug" Clyde decided, removing the gag and carving a Glasgow smile into the man's face.

"I'm sorry" Connor yelled pitifully, "I won't tell anyone". Clyde smiled at him and asked, "what's the fun in that?". "How could I rape anyone with no fingers and no dick?" Connor asked before sobbing, "I'll never do anything like that ever again". Clyde debated it. What the man said did make sense but at this point he knew it was him and he was going to squeal to the cops.

"I'll take you to the hospital under one circumstance" Clyde said. Connor perked up and looked at him hopefully. "If I can cut out your tongue" Clyde told him. "You sick bastard," Connor cried, "I said I wouldn't tell anyone!". "I don't trust you" Clyde shrugged before asking, "so what will it be?". Connor didn't answer, he simply screamed and sobbed.

"Fuck me eyes" Clyde said angrily before musing, "maybe your eyes should go next". Clyde headed to Connor's room and returned with a bag of instruments. "Once your eye is out, I'll let you leave" Clyde smiled, grabbing a scalpel. Connor screamed in agony when the instrument was stuck into his skull. "Why'd you give me fuck me eyes, Connor?" Clyde asked, mimicking him. By the time the eye was fully out the man was limp and he was no longer screaming.

"I thought you were stronger" Clyde shrugged before removing the other eye and his heart. He tore open the man's stomach and grabbed a few other organs. He looked around Connor's house and found a box that he'd seemingly gotten on either Christmas or his birthday. *From: mom, To: Connor.* Perfect. Clyde packaged the removed appendages and organs into the pretty box.

He looked around for something to start a fire. He found gasoline and matches. He poured gasoline all over the office and Connor's bedroom before setting the house ablaze. He then drove to Cora's mother's house where he left the box in front of her door, knowing that she'd see it when she went to get her daily newspaper.

Detective

Cora woke up in the morning to her mother's phone call. The frantic woman was screaming and crying telling her to come over. Cora woke Clyde up and told him that they'd have to go. Clyde drove her over and they saw the old woman crying in an officer's arms. "What happened?" Cora asked. "Connor died," Crystal sobbed, smoking a cigarette. "How?" Clyde asked. "I don't know exactly how b-but they cut off his penis, finger, tongue. They removed his eyes and heart...they were left in a gift box on my doorstep".

Cora hugged her mother as tears welled up in her own eyes. "His house was also set on fire after the fact" an officer told her. "Who could be that cruel?" Cora asked, looking disgusted. "I don't know," Crystal said, "but whoever it is, needs to pay". Clyde joined the mother and daughter in a group hug and gave them condolences for their loss. "You didn't even like Connor," Crystal cried softly. "Doesn't mean he can't be sad, mom," Cora argued. "Do you think it was the serial killer?" Clyde asked the officers. "We don't think so, this isn't his MO. We think this was a personal attack".

Cora opted for not going to work. "Why are you crying?" Clyde asked when he looked over at her. "What the fuck is wrong with you?" Cora asked before crying, "my brother just died". "The same brother that called you a whore and tried to rape you" Clyde pointed out. He swerved into another lane and almost hit a truck head on when Cora slapped him. "Pull over!" she screamed. "What? No!" Clyde yelled back, driving faster. Cora screamed at the top of her lungs and began to fight him. Clyde veered off the road and hit a tree.

"What the fuck, Cora?" he hissed as she got out of the car. "You don't even care that my brother just died," Cora cried, walking down the street. "Where the fuck are you going?" Clyde asked, following her in his car. "Don't worry about it" Cora sobbed. "Go get the car fixed" she screamed at him. Before Clyde could retort, thunder clapped and it began to rain. "Cora, don't be like this. Get in the car" Clyde coaxed. "Leave me alone," Cora screamed. At this point everyone was staring at them. Clyde reluctantly drove away.

Cora walked for a few miles until she saw a sign saying that the hospital was a mile away. She hugged herself as the wind blew. It was cold and rainy. She was almost to the hospital when a man dressed in all black tried to grab her. She fought him away and ran as fast as she could. When she made it inside the hospital, she was panting. "Are you okay?" security asked her, concerned. "I need to see my friend," Cora said, breathing heavily. The security officer nodded, checked her and let her through. After talking to the lady at the front desk, she was given a visitor pass that didn't stick to her damp clothing and escorted to the room.

Preston sat up and grinned when he saw her. "Hey," Preston smiled. "Hey" Cora said sadly before telling him, "Connor died". Preston's smile fell and he asked, "how?". Cora felt like throwing up again as tears rolled down her cheeks. "His dick, heart, tongue and fingers were removed" she said, sitting on the edge of Preston's bed. He rubbed her back comfortingly. "And then I got attacked on the way over here" she cried. "By a man wearing all black?" he asked. "How did you know?" Cora gasped. "Same guy attacked me".

Preston took his thin hospital blanket and wrapped it around her. "Thank you" Cora smiled. "Of course," Preston grinned at her. "I miss this," Preston commented. "Miss what?" Cora asked. "Having moments like this with you" Preston sighed, "but I messed it up". "Clyde showed his true colors today" Cora sighed, "he was happy that Connor died". "I'm sorry about that," Preston frowned. "It's okay," Cora said looking at him. The duo lingered eye contact until Preston worked up the courage to lean in and kiss her.

"I'm engaged," Cora squeaked, standing up. "He doesn't have to know," Preston argued. Cora's heart was racing and she debated on what to do. She couldn't call Clyde after how he acted towards her earlier and her mother had the tendency to be abusive. She reluctantly sat back on the edge of the bed. "Don't do that again," Cora told him. "Why are you smiling then?" Preston asked. "I didn't say I didn't like it" Cora said, "I said don't do it again. It's a difference". Preston smiled at her. "So what are you gonna do?" Preston asked. "I'm gonna unmask the killer" Cora said, "finally find out who it is".

"Wait until I'm discharged" Preston told her, "I don't want you to get attacked and I'm not there to protect you". Cora nodded. "Can I do it again?" Preston asked shyly. Cora was confused until she laughed and pulled him in for a kiss. She straddled his lap and made out with him. "Fuck, I've missed this" Preston groaned, resting his forehead on hers. "Me too," Cora hummed. Preston made her giggle by pressing kisses all over her damp cheeks.

They were interrupted when there was a knock on the door. Cora quickly slid into a chair adjacent to the bed as the door swung open. A nurse was accompanied by Clyde holding a large bouquet of daisies. "Hey" Cora said, looking at him. "Brought these for you" Clyde told Preston, holding them in front of him so that he could smell them. "Allergic" Preston hissed. "Forgot" Clyde shrugged before fixing his gaze on Cora and asking, "do you want them?". "Sure" she said, reluctantly accepting them.

Clyde leaned in to kiss her but she pushed him away. "You're still mad?" Clyde asked. "I know it's you, Clyde" Preston hissed, "you even tried to attack poor Cora on the way here". Clyde looked at them in confusion and asked, "what?". "You wore your little black outfit and attacked her," Preston hissed. Clyde's blood ran cold. "I've been at the dealership all day," he said honestly. "The alibi checks out" Cora agreed.

Preston's face turned to one of horror. If Clyde was accounted for all day, that meant that someone else was out there. Perhaps a copycat. He tried to keep his composure in front of the couple. "We'll get down to the bottom of it together" Clyde decided. Preston looked at him skeptically but agreed for Cora's sake. "How long until you're discharged?" Clyde asked. "Few days," Preston said. "When you get discharged, we can find the guy," Clyde smiled. Preston simply stared at him. "Ready to go, babe?" Clyde asked, turning to Cora. Cora hesitantly nodded and bid Preston goodbye.

Stand Off

When Clyde woke up in the morning, Cora was snuggling with Preston. He grimaced at the scene but decided not to cause a scene in public. He clicked on the television and saw Seth presenting the news. There had been two more people killed in just one night. He shook the duo awake. Cora and Preston both eyes the screen warily. After a few minutes, a doctor came in and discharged the anchor.

When Preston got discharged, Clyde and Cora gave him a ride home. When they got to Preston's house, he broke out a notepad and pen. "So what's the plan?" the blonde asked. "We could let the cops do their job," Clyde shrugged. Cora laughed at that and said, "I have a plan". "What is it?" Clyde asked. "I'm not telling," she said. Clyde raised an eyebrow but Preston just said, "I think we all need to stay together. Splitting up won't do us any good". "No offense, dude, but I don't want to stay with you" Clyde laughed before getting up to leave. "Sit the fuck down" Preston commanded, pointing a gun at him.

"Put the gun down," Cora sighed. Clyde sat down and Preston said, "I'm going to call Seth and a few others to come over. They can help us brainstorm". "This is stupid" Clyde hissed. "Why are you so worried?" Preston asked before whispering, "unless you're the killer". "Clyde's not the killer" Cora argued softly. "You don't know that, Cora," Preston told her. He set his phone down and said, "everyone's coming to sleep over. You guys can go home to grab some stuff but I expect you to be back".

When the couple went home, Cora saw Clyde packing a gun and a knife. "What do you need that for?" she asked. "To even the score" Clyde shrugged, "if Preston's gonna be armed, I will too". Cora rolled her eyes and said, "you're being ridiculous". Clyde packed his recording equipment before he was ready to leave. "I need a weapon too" Cora said suddenly as they were driving to Preston's place. "I thought I was being ridiculous," Clyde mimicked. Despite his words, he reached into the console of his car and handed her a knife. Cora eyed it skeptically. It smelled strongly of cleaner.

When they got back to Preston's house, they saw a few cars that they didn't recognize parked on the grass and driveway. Clyde hesitantly knocked and Preston immediately greeted them. Clyde looked over and saw a few of the camera crew from the station. "What's the plan?" Clyde asked. "No plan," Preston smiled. While Cora sat on the couch with Preston, Seth loudly asked, "Hey, new kid, can you grab me a beer?". "I don't see any," Clyde said, eyeing the fridge skeptically. Seth pulled Clyde aside and whispered, "Preston thinks the killer is in the house. So he's going to keep us from leaving".

"What the fuck" Clyde cursed. "He's really lost it" Seth agreed before saying, "let's promise to stick together if shit hits the fan". "Of course" Clyde promised before asking, "where were you yesterday?". Seth named a local restaurant before returning to the living room. Clyde's blood ran cold when he thought about their hours of operation. They weren't open yesterday. He cursed silently, he needed to get Cora out of here. He headed back into the living room and squeezed on the couch in between her and Preston.

"Someone died yesterday," Preston announced. "You know it wasn't me or Cora because we stayed with you all night" Clyde pointed out. Preston nodded before checking everyone's alibis. Seth said that he was at a grocery store. "I thought you said restaurant," Clyde said, calling him out in front of everyone. Preston raised an eyebrow at his co-star. "I misspoke earlier" Seth said, glaring at Clyde. The camera crew recorded every second. "This is fucking stupid" Seth hissed. "You got any better ideas?" Preston asked.

"It's like an adult sleepover," Cora sang. "Precisely" Preston agreed, pulling out board games. Clyde and Seth both hesitantly joined them on the floor. They all sat in a circle around the coffee table. "This is fucking stupid" Seth hissed, throwing his cards down. "Stop it," Preston scolded. "I agree," Clyde said, putting his cards down. The duo left in separate directions and the recording crew followed them. "So it's just me and you," Preston smiled. "I guess so," Cora said, smiling shyly. She sat with her knees hugged to her chest and her arms around her knees.

"Why are you so far away?" Preston asked. Cora rolled her eyes before crawling beside him. "So why are we here?" Cora asked. "I think Seth and Clyde are killers" Preston whispered, "we just need to get the evidence on the camera". When Cora went to move away, Preston pulled her back. "I promise you" he insisted, "the guy that attacked me was the same build as Clyde. And let's be real if a guy was trying to attack you yesterday- he could easily overpower you if he wanted. He probably stopped because he recognized you".

Cora moved closer to Preston in fear when the lights turned off. "It's okay, I'll protect you" he told her before getting up to check. Cora hid behind him as they headed to the breaker. Cora let out a scream when she stepped in something wet. Preston clasped a hand over her mouth. He shined his flashlight and saw that the pool of liquid was red. "Shit" he cursed. Cora began to hyperventilate. They stepped over the pool of liquid and went to find everyone else. "C'mon" Preston said, pulling her by her arm upstairs.

They headed into his bedroom to stay safe. Preston locked and barricaded the door. "So what now?" Cora asked. "We need to call the cops" Preston looked for his phone and cursed. "Do you have your phone?" he asked Cora. "Clyde took it," Cora sighed. "Fuck" Preston sighed. "Are we screwed?" Cora asked. "No, I have my gun," he told her. Cora slumped onto his bed. "So what now?" she asked. "I can think of something to kill time," Preston said huskily. "That was a one time thing" Cora argued.

"He left you Cora" Preston told her, "he knows there's potentially a killer in this house and he left you. So he either doesn't care about you or he knows you're safe because he's the killer". Cora exhaled deeply. "I just want to protect you" Preston promised her, reaching out and leaning in to kiss her. Cora pushed him back and dodged the kiss. "Cora, I love you"

Preston told her. "I love you too but I'm engaged" Cory sighed. Preston reached into his nightstand and pulled out a diamond ring.

"I can propose to you," he smiled. Cora took the ring and gasped. "It's beautiful," she told him. "I know, beautiful just like you" Preston smiled, "we can get married, have a family. You just have to ditch that fucking psychopath". Cora looked like she was debating it. She stood up and wrapped her arms around him, giving him a chaste kiss. "Let's kill some time," she smiled. Preston laughed and wrapped his hands around her waist.

Preston pulled his pants back up and gave Cora one more kiss before he left the room. Cora followed closely behind him. "Try to be as quiet as possible," he told her. "Where were you guys?" Seth asked, appearing from the darkness. "Looking for you," Preston lied. "They're dead," Seth said. "Who?" Preston asked. "The camera crew. Clyde killed them" Seth said, gasping. "Why are you covered in blood?" Preston asked. "I was checking for a pulse," Seth said.

Seth's face and clothing were splattered with blood. "I tried to help them," Seth said, walking towards the duo. They both backed up and Preston drew his gun. "I'm not the killer, Preston," Seth told him, "it's Clyde". "Get on the floor" Preston said, gesturing down with the gun. Seth slowly got down on the floor. When Preston approached to check his person, Seth slashed his leg. Preston immediately fired six rounds into the man's head. "Fuck" Preston hissed in pain. Thankfully, the meteorologist missed his Achilles tendon.

They retreated into the bathroom where Cora wrapped his leg. They heard pounding on the door. Cora hid in the tub with the curtain drawn closed. Preston held his gun at the door that was being kicked in with each knock. Preston didn't know what to do so he shot through the door. The knocking stopped. Preston limped to the door and opened it. When he looked down, he saw a member of the film crew. "Shit" Preston cursed. "It was you?" the man on the ground asked, coughing up blood.

"We need to leave," Preston told Cora, grabbing her and heading downstairs. They headed outside and Preston saw that all four of his tires were slashed. "Fuck it" Preston said as they got inside. It was raining and thundering. Preston hit the gas and tried to drive off but the car wouldn't start. "We need to head back inside" he told Cora, "we're sitting ducks out here". "I'm scared," Cora said with tears rolling down her cheeks. "You have to be strong," Preston told her.

"We just have to find my phone," Preston told her. "If we can find Clyde, he has my phone," Cora told him. "Stay close," Preston told her. They headed back inside and went to look for Clyde. Preston cautiously opened each door on the first floor. He hesitantly headed upstairs. He checked every room and didn't see Clyde. Preston headed into the attic but the new hire was nowhere to be seen. "I can pretend to be hurt to lure him out," Cora suggested through her tears. "It's too risky," Preston argued. "We have to try," Cora insisted.

Preston dampened a wrap with Seth's blood and tied it around Cora's legs. Cora lay on the living room floor and screamed for help. "Help me! Please!" Cora cried. She screamed for half an hour before Clyde came inside. He was drenched from the rain and his eyes were dark. "Baby, what happened?" Clyde asked, dropping to his knees. "I got shot," Cora hissed. Clyde looked at her and smiled. "Preston shot you after you fucked him?" Clyde asked. Cora stared up at him, her heart beating. "I loved you, Cora," Clyde said, pulling out his gun. Tears rolled down her cheeks. Right when Clyde was about to shoot his fiance, Preston shot him through his left eye.

"You never loved me" Clyde hissed, reeling in pain on the floor. He picked up his gun and fired a few shots in Preston's direction. Cora grabbed her knife and stabbed her fiance. Clyde grabbed his gun and shot her in the stomach. Cora continued stabbing him until he was limp. Preston ran downstairs and fired a few shots into Clyde's unmoving skull. Cora heaved in pain, blood pouring from her mouth. Blood was splattered all over her face and clothing.

Preston looked through Clyde's pocket and called the police. He carried Cora bridal style upstairs and placed her on the closed toilet lid. He went to his bedroom and took off her engagement ring. He replaced it with the ring that he bought for her and kissed her forehead. Tears of pain rolled down Cora's face. "It'll be okay" he promised her. He pressed kisses to her cheek as he used his hands to keep pressure on her wounds. Preston rested his forehead on hers until they heard sirens in the distance.

Epilogue

"My name is Coraline Katz and I'm signing on with Channel Five News," Cora smiled, "today I have some big news to share. I'm pregnant". She unbuttoned her blazer and revealed a belly bump in her white blouse. She rubbed her stomach and smiled. "I did that," Preston said, causing her to laugh before she forced a poker face. "We're on air" she said, swatting his roaming hand away. She finished the rest of her report without incident.

"This is Coraline Katz and we're signing off with Channel Five News" she sang. When she stopped filming, Preston gave her a kiss. "I love you" he told her. "I love you too," Cora smiled. He carried her out to his sports car. Cora giggled and smiled. "I want to visit my mom," she told him. Preston nodded and drove to the rehab center. They'd given the woman the ultimatum that if she wanted to be in her grandchild's life that she'd have to go to rehab.

They grabbed flowers before heading to the center. The duo got checked in and headed to the woman's room. Crystal immediately ran over to her daughter and hugged her. "I've missed you," the blonde cooed before rubbing her daughter's stomach. "Did you find out the gender yet?" the older woman asked. "You're trying to decide if you hate it or not?" Preston quipped. "Stop it" Cora scolded, lightly nudging him. "We're waiting until birth to find out the gender" Cora answers.

"How are you feeling?" Preston asked. "Good, considering I haven't had a drink in months and my son died," Crystal said. Cora frowned at that statement. The young woman rubbed her mother's back soothingly and said, "I have a feeling it's a girl". "Would you like to go for lunch with us?" Preston asked. "If the nurses will let me," Crystal laughed. "I can bribe them," he winked. Crystal laughed. Cora took her mother's hand and the trio headed off into the sunset.

www.ingramcontent.com/pod-product-compliance
Lightning Source LLC
Chambersburg PA
CBHW021321160726
47994CB00004B/1546